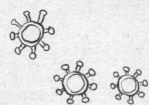

When Mom's Away

Layla Ahmad
Farida Zaman

Second Story Press

I smile as Mom gives me breakfast—cereal, an egg, and juice—just the way I like it, the same every day. I stop smiling when she tells me her news.

"I have to be away again for a little bit…well, not really away… but not in the house with you and Daddy."

"Why?" I ask, feeling like I might not like this at all.

"We hoped it would slow down, but the virus is spreading again and sending lots of people to the hospital," says Mom. "It's my job to help them get well."

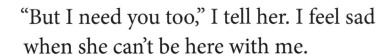

"I wish you could stay at home!" I say.

"I don't want you and Daddy to catch the virus."

"What if the virus makes you sick?" I say, feeling scared.

Mom hugs me. "Try not to worry. I'll do everything I can to stay safe. I'll wear gloves and masks and wash my hands. The people in the hospital need me."

"But I need you too," I tell her. I feel sad when she can't be here with me.

"I know," she says. "And I'll be back before you know it. In the meantime, your dad will do a great job looking after you."

Mom, Dad, and I spend the morning making sure Mom has everything she needs in the garage, where she sleeps when she has to stay away from us. We bring all the things Mom needs to feel comfortable. There is even a little table with a reading light and a picture of the three of us.

"There!" Mom says when we're finished. "It's almost like camping out."

Later on, Mom gives Dad and me big hugs and kisses and leaves for work.

I can't help it. I cry a little. It's not the same without her.

"It's just two of us for a while, kiddo," Dad says. "But we can make Mom's job easier while she's busy being a superhero."

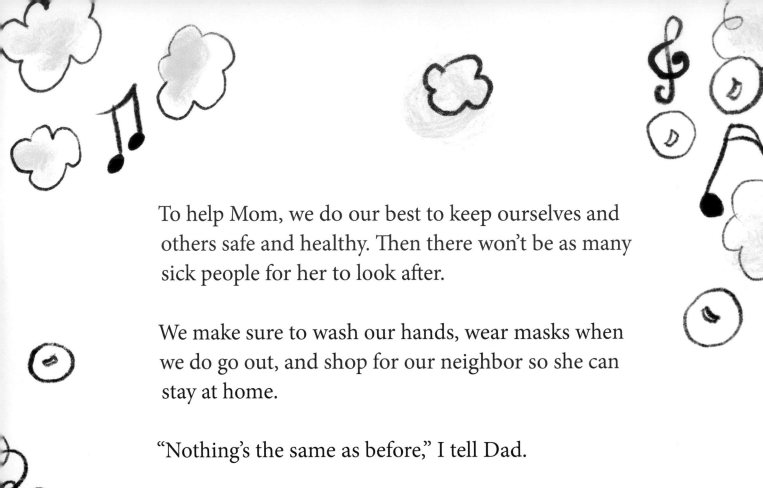

To help Mom, we do our best to keep ourselves and others safe and healthy. Then there won't be as many sick people for her to look after.

We make sure to wash our hands, wear masks when we do go out, and shop for our neighbor so she can stay at home.

"Nothing's the same as before," I tell Dad.

"No, but it's still pretty good." Dad ruffles my hair. "Come on. Let's sing a special hand-washing song and clean up for dinner."

Singing loudly makes us hungry!

We look in the pantry and use things we already have.
Dad says Mommy would like that.

It's fun to help cook. Dad often cooks anyway since
Mom is a busy doctor!

Later the phone rings, and it's a video chat just for me!

It's Mom!

I tell her I miss her, but I know it's important to help people get better. I stand extra tall when she says, "That's my big girl. I'm so proud of you!"

Every morning, Dad helps me get dressed. He braids my hair. He tries hard, but it's not the same. I don't tell him, though, I just think it.

I go to school on the computer. I see my friends from my class on the screen with my teacher. I try hard, but it isn't the same, either. I miss my teacher and my friends!

Every evening, I wait by the window so I can see Mom come home and go straight to the garage. I draw a heart on the window to show I love her. She is a superhero. She's helping her patients get better.

Daddy and I want to be like
Mom and help people too.

We go grocery shopping for
Grandma and Grandpa,
and then deliver their food.
We have to stay outside, just
like Mom. I give a big wave,
so they know it's me.

Sometimes before dinner, our neighbors stand outside and clap for my mom and all the other superheroes just like her. Some bang on pots and pans, some even sing. I shout the loudest. Maybe Mommy can hear me!

The days pass quickly because we're so busy! And now, I can hardly sleep! Mom's coming back home soon!!!

When I wake up, it's not the same…. It's even better!
Mom is right here, hugging me.

"Is the virus gone?" I ask.

"No, but there aren't as many sick people in the
hospital. Things are getting better."

Mom tells me she'll have to go back to work in a while,
but for now, it's the three of us again—just the way
I like it.

"I missed you so much," Mom tells Dad and me.
"Thank you both for doing such a good job while
I was away."

She laughs when I say, "No problem, Mom.
That's what superheroes do!"

To every teacher at home and in the classroom.
—L.A.

For children everywhere.
—F.Z.

Library and Archives Canada Cataloguing in Publication

Title: When Mom's away / Layla Ahmad ; [illustrated by] Farida Zaman.
Names: Ahmad, Layla, 1992- author. | Zaman, Farida, illustrator.
Identifiers: Canadiana 20200333836 | ISBN 9781772601756 (hardcover)
Classification: LCC PS8601.H56 W54 2021 | DDC jC813/.6—dc23

Printed and bound in China

*Second Story Press gratefully acknowledges the support of the Ontario Arts Council
and the Canada Council for the Arts for our publishing program. We acknowledge the
financial support of the Government of Canada through the Canada Book Fund.*

 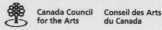

ONTARIO ARTS COUNCIL
CONSEIL DES ARTS DE L'ONTARIO
an Ontario government agency
un organisme du gouvernement de l'Ontario

Canada Council   Conseil des Arts
for the Arts   du Canada

Funded by the   Financé par le
Government   gouvernement
of Canada   du Canada

Canada

Published by
Second Story Press
20 Maud Street, Suite 401
Toronto, Ontario, Canada
M5V 2M5
www.secondstorypress.ca